MINE

KAY MAREE

1

Contents

Petal, Mine
All rights reserved

Copyright © 2018 by Kay Maree

Cover Design © Designed With Grace - http://www.designedwgrace.com/
Cover Images © Adobe Stock & Deposit Photos
Editing – Susan Horsnell & Word Writer Pro

About the Author

I live in Newcastle, on the New South Wales coast of Australia with my husband and three beautiful children.

Between being a taxi for my children, and working full-time, I somehow find the time to write. It's something I love with a passion and with the encouragement of my very supportive husband, I have accomplished one of my dreams – releasing my first novel.

I hope you fall in love with my characters as much as I have.

I love reading and getting lost in a good book when I manage to snatch five minutes to myself.

Kay Maree

I dedicate this to all my ladies that wanted more of the Grasso men and their woman xx

To all the ladies that are new to me, welcome to my world and I have one question for you.....

Do you believe in Love at first sight???

Social Links

Facebook:
https://www.facebook.com/kay.maree.334
Twitter:
https://twitter.com/MisKay85
Goodreads:
https://www.goodreads.com/book/show/34528910-
angel-mine?ac=1&from_search=true
Goodreads Author Page:
https://www.goodreads.com/user/show/65394903-kay-
maree

Chapter One

Nico

I cringe at the sound coming from my night stand, it's loud enough to wake the fucken dead. Cursing as I roll over, why? Why didn't I silence it when I crawled into bed? I run a hand down the side of my face to calm my frayed nerves, fuck I'm tired. When I take a glance at the clock on my bedside table, the illuminated figures show it's 6 am. It's barely light out.

I reach out and search blindly for my phone, which I locate next to the clock. Antonio's name flashes on the screen. Shit, I hit the button to receive the call.

"Capo Bastone." Shit my voice sounds raspy and tired as hell.

"Nico, you need to get your ass down to Destiny. Now!"

"Why? I didn't leave there until two this morning. What's happened?" Sitting up, I lower my feet onto the carpeted floor. Not wanting to move, my muscles protest.

"Stop asking fucking questions, Fanculo (fuck), just get here."

"Si." the dial tone in my ear informs me that he didn't even wait for my reply.

He's pissed, I could feel it burning off him and through the phone. Great! What a fucken great way to start the day. What the hell could have happened at Destiny?

I drag my tired hand over my face wiping away the sleep I still wish I was in. Reaching out, I pick up the framed photo of my beautiful woman. The images of her assault my mind every morning I do this and I wish I was waking up with her laying next to me in our bed, not on my nightstand in a fucken photo frame. I run my fingertips over the glass and bless her, it's a ritual I perform every day without fail. If I'm away from home on a job, the photo goes with me. My heart squeezes in my chest as flashes assault my mind from the day which changed my world forever.

After dragging my fingers through my hair, I reach for the shorts I'd dropped on the floor a few hours earlier. I pull them onto my tired body and slip on a tee which had been on the floor also. It smells a bit but a spray of cologne and I'll be good to go. Shit, if Antonio is forced to wait longer than he deems okay, he'll go from irate to erupting volcano in the blink of an eye.

***

It's barely light out when I pull up to the front of Destiny. The telltale red and blue lights of fire trucks light up the early dawn sky. What the fuck? My mind races as I pull up behind one of the fire trucks and slam the car into park before killing the engine. After stepping from the car, I walk down the side of the fire truck. *What the fuck is happening?* I run my fingers over the shiny red truck, dread hitting the pit of my stomach when I see Antonio talking to a firefighter.

"Capo Bastone, what the fuck happened" I look around, the front of the building doesn't look that bad.

"I was going to ask you the same question." His voice has an edge which puts me on guard straight away.

I drag my fingers through my already unruly hair. Before I can say anything, Antonio pulls his phone out and starts to turn away.

"Antonio?"

"Nico, you need to get your shit together and stop fucking around. A lot of shit is going down right now and I need you to be on your fucking game, not focused on the latest pussy your sticking your dick into."

Whoa where the fuck did that come from? I open my mouth to answer my irate boss. "Si." Is the only word I utter, no point pissing him off further.

Lifting his chin, he holds the phone to his ear and heads to the back of Destiny, I follow behind.

"Boss, there has been a fire at Destiny," Antonio says into his phone, I tune out the rest of the conversation as I look at the damage at the back of the building. My body is shaking and it's not caused by the new dawn's chill. I clench my knuckles until they turn white and fingernails bite into the flesh of my closed fist.

"Figlio di puttana." (son of a bitch)

"What Fratello?" Antonio growls as he come up behind me.

"That piece of shit MC club," I snap when I see the red spray paint all over the old maintenance shed. Shaking my head, anger sparks like a broken cable off me.

"Dom's going to want blood for this, Nico. We need to find fucking answers before the Boss turns up." Antonio's voice is cold and laced with anger even to my ears.

Paybacks always a bitch and these fuckers will definitely pay for what they have done. You don't fuck with Grasso's and get away with it.

The screeching of tyres draws my attention to the front of the building. Mickey stops the car and Dom climbs out of the passenger side. The clipped sound of his shoes on the concrete pulls my attention towards my boss. I see the annoyance and anger radiating off him and instinctively take a step back.

I watch Dom slam his fist into his pocket and pull his phone free. He punches in a number and I know who he is calling - Sergio. All hell is going to break loose and the storm known as *The House of Grasso* will rain down on this town and the MC motherfuckers.

Doms voice is calm but clipped as he fills Sergio in.

"Sergio, some cazzo set fire to Destiny, I need you to meet me here." There's a pause while he listens before speaking again. "Si, I think it has to do with Demetri's Butterfly."

I pace back and forth, I'm jacked up on adrenaline and nerves mixed with next to no sleep.

"I'll explain more when you get here. Make sure Theo keeps his eyes on Kirsty. Mickey is on his way to keep watch out the front." Dominic ends the call and shoves the phone back in his pocket.

"This is plain fucking retaliation for Demetri and his butterfly." Dominic's voice cuts through my thoughts.

"Antonio, we need to get control of this shit."

"Si Boss, I'll get Johnny digging up everything on these fuckers."

"Bene," Dom says as his phone starts to ring.

"Angel." Dom moves away.

"Antonio, let's check what we can save." He nods and we head towards the worst of it to start looking around while we wait for Dominic.

***

Fifteen minutes later Sergio pulls up, jumps out of his car and heads towards us

"Boss," he greets before lifting his chin to me and Antonio.

"About fucking time, Sergio," Dom snaps, anger rolling off him in waves.

"How's Kirsty?" Antonio asks.

"Better." He smiles making me and Antonio chuckle.

"We need to get a handle on this shit." Dom snaps while running a hand through his hair.

"Why do you think it has something to do with the woman Demetri has?" Sergio asks.

Dominic doesn't say a word. We follow him as he walks around a corner to the back of the building where the small maintenance shed is and points towards the symbol for the motorcycle club spray painted on the shed.

"Fanculo!" Sergio growls.

Dominic turns to face us and points at Sergio. "You and me are going to see Demetri while Antonio and Nico clean up this fucking mess." Anger rolls off him in waves.

Sergio nods heads back to his car. Dominic follows him and shouts over his shoulder to Antonio but doesn't stop walking.

"I want fucking answers, Antonio."

"Si, Boss."

"Nico let's get this shit cleaned up," Antonio growls.

10

I head to get cleaning supplies from the shed.

Bucket of hot water and soap? Nope that shit won't work. I search the shed and find a bottle of turps which I grab along with the bucket and a few rags. I also snatch two brooms which are leaning against the wall. I hand one of the brooms to Antonio and fill the bucket with turps. After dipping my broom into the liquid, I shake off the excess and raise it to the angry red MC logo which has been haphazardly plastered over the shed doors. As I scrub, the red paint appears to magically disappear as red streaks run down the doors.

"What a fucken mess," I growl.

"You can say that again, fratello." He drops his broom into the bucket and wipes his arm across his forehead.

"Go home, brother, it's been a long night for you and it's going to be a long day for all of us." His tired and black ringed eyes fix on my face. "Are you sure?" He raises an eyebrow at me.

"Yeah, fuck off home. I can't fuck up this shit, it's already a mess. Your shoulder is still messed up, you should be resting it."

He shrugs and throws one of the rags at me before turning and walking away. "See you soon."

I chuckle and finish scrubbing the last of the paint off. I fill the bucket with hot water four times and douse the doors, removing the last remnants. I stand back satisfied, there is no trace of the logo.

Sweat beads on my forehead and drops slide down my spine. I glance up at the sky, the sun is out and blazing down on me. I reckon it must be after nine by now. I head back to the shed and put everything back in it's place. As I secure the door, something off to one side catches my eye. I lock the doors and head for the back of the shed where the skip bins are kept. When I crouch down, I see a small, very small pair of dirty, bare feet peeking out from behind. Standing, I slide a skip bin out of the way which reveals the tiny, dirty frame of a woman. She stares up at me, eyes full of terror, shaking like a leaf. I crouch down again and her hands rise in a defensive position. I raise my hands in an attempt to show her I mean her no harm.

"Please, please, leave me alone." Her voice is husky but as soft as a summer wind.

"I won't hurt you." I speak quietly in an attempt to reassure her. The girl's terror filled eyes watch every move I make and I notice amongst the dirt and filth of her face, they are an amazing shade of brown.

I shimmy a fraction closer and drop to my knees. Even though I keep my movements slow, she backs further away from me. When her back hits the brick wall, she has nowhere to go.

"Babe, what's your name?"

I slip my hand into my short's pocket, pushing the keys and phone out of my way and feel the Granola bar I'd put in there last night to quell my hunger during the night shift. When my fingers lock around it, I take it out and hold it toward the terrified girl.

"Here, babe, take it."

I keep my voice as soft as I possibly can which is difficult when I want to scream and rant about how a stunning little lady like her could be living on the streets. It appears she has been doing so for a while.

"Babe, please take it, it looks like you need it."

A weak smile kisses her lips which have a plump, sexy cupid's bow. I nudge the bar closer and her scared eyes meet mine. Rage fills me to my very core at her situation. She extends a shaky hand and takes the bar in long, thin fingers. When her grimy digits brush against my strong, clean ones, a strong current shoots through me. I snap my hand back so fast it causes her to start and she drops the bar. Her hands fly to her face and she buries her head in them and sobs.

"Shit. Fuck, babe, I'm sorry. It's just I haven't felt anything like that for a very long time." I rub my palm over my tired face.

"The filth on me?"

The weight of her words hit me with the force of a truck. "Fuck, babe. That's absolutely not what I meant." My voice is gravelly with emotion. I keep an eye on her as I pick up the bar and hand it back to her. "What's a pretty little thing like you doing here?"

She takes the bar again, being careful not to touch me again. I'm thankful for that because right at this moment all I want to do is take her tiny body in my arms and make her feel safe.

"I live here."

"Here? As in behind the club?"

"Yes," she says as she crunches on the bar.

"For how long?"

"About a week. I had to move from the train station."

Fuck me. I try to wrap my head around this shit. I sit back on my heels and watch her eat, the way her jaw moves as she bites down. Her matted black hair falls around her face. Shit, she's so beautiful despite the dirt of street living.

"I'm going to take you somewhere safe, babe. You can have a shower, get cleaned up and have a decent meal." My voice is a bit harsher than I intend and she cringes away from me.

"Um, no you're not." Her tiny voice snaps at me.

A chuckle bubbles in my throat at the sound of strength in her voice, such a tiny human facing off with a man like me. Strength is not something I would have thought she had in her.

"Yes, I am, babe. I'm not leaving you on the streets."

She shakes her head defiantly, her large brown eyes fixed on me and the terror from earlier is almost gone. "No, I'm not. Thanks for the bar but....."

She pushes herself onto shaky feet and when she stumbles backwards, my arms fly out instinctively and wrap around her waist. I hold her in place, a shock passes through me like before and rocks me to the core. *What the fuck is happening to me?*

I shake away my thoughts and concentrate on preventing her from falling. She's so delicate, petite. She reminds me of the flowers Brooklyn decorates hers and Dom's home with.

I clear my throat. "You are coming with me. You will allow me to take care of you. It's not up for discussion. Sorry, but I won't allow you to remain on the streets, half starved."

My voice sounds a little shaky to my ears as I struggle to control myself. Holding her close, I feel every stuttered breath she takes and notice how dark her eyes actually are. They remind me of rich coffee and hold me hypnotized for a moment. When I take a deep breath and hold her tighter, I feel her freeze.

"Breathe, babe." She gazes at me with a deer caught in headlights expression.

"You don't even know me."

"I don't need to know you to be able to see you need me." I scoop her into my arms and close to my chest. As I head for my car, I feel her shaking. I'm unsure if it's because she's cold or if it's shock from me picking her up without warning.

I fish the keys from pocket and push the remote button to unlock the doors. The beep sounds overly loud in the quiet of the alley. She flinches and her eyes slam shut at the sound. I hold her closer.

"Sssh, it's okay. I won't let anything hurt you."

I pop the boot of the car and grab a jacket I keep there. After sitting her into the passenger seat, I wrap her tiny body in the jacket which engulfs her. She snuggles into the fabric, closes her eyes and a small smile kisses her beautiful lips.

Shocking myself, I lean forward and place a kiss to her forehead, she has the softest skin I have ever felt. She jerks away from my touch and I grit my teeth against stopping her. I blow out a deep breath and rein in the temptation to do it again.

"Sorry," I murmur. I want to punch myself in the face for allowing these feelings to take over. I need to keep my guard up because I don't have time to be distracted by this shit. Shit is so much simpler when feelings aren't involved and no-one gets hurt. I need to remind myself of this. Images of the last time I felt this way flash through my mind and my gut twists.

I strap the seatbelt around her, close the door and head to the driver's side. Bracing my hands on the roof, I lower my head and take several deep breaths.

Get your shit together, this is why I fuck and leave. I will not allow this girl to get to me. I'll take her home, get her cleaned up and then call Brooklyn to ask if she can stay with them until she's back on her feet. Even I can feel what a fucking lie the thoughts are. One touch. One fucking touch and I feel like I'm addicted. I need more, so much fucking more from this delicate flower.

I slide into the car and look across at her.

"Please let me take care of you, Petal." I say the words before thinking and see a flash of fear cross her eyes but there's a touch of warmth which wasn't there before.

"Okay," she whispers before turning to look out the window.

Yeah, I'm fucked. Less than thirty minutes I've known her and I don't think I could let her go even if I wanted to.

Chapter Two

Josie

What the hell just happened? It felt like every single one of my nerve endings had been electrified. My skin was hypersensitized by his touch. I've never felt anything like it and if I'm being completely honest, it scares the shit out of me. I need to fight it, I can't allow it to affect me. I can't think about how the sound of his gravelly voice raced down my spine and caused goosebumps to break out over my skin or the sight of his silver eyes piercing through me. I've never seen eyes like his. They seemed to lock onto every move I made. Studied every breath I took. I can't, no – I won't allow them to capture me. I need to be strong and push through the feelings. I can't allow myself to be taken on another emotional rollercoaster and I have a feeling if I let this man get close, he will break what's left of me.

I'll take his kindness for what it is and maybe he can help me get back what I've lost. So, no – I won't think about how I felt when I was in his arms, how safe he makes me feel.

I'll continue staring through the window and watching the scenery speed past. I should be scared, I have no idea where he's taking me but there was something in his eyes which reassured me and the way he said, *I won't hurt you*, made me believe he won't.

"I don't need your help," I snap and immediately feel guilty for speaking that way. He's only attempting to help me but being in a closed car with him with his scent surrounding me makes my head spin. I open my mouth to apologize but he speaks first.

"What's your name, Petal?"

His smooth, accented voice adds to my inner turmoil and I debate about whether or not to tell him the truth. In the end I can't lie.

"Josie." I study his face out of the corner of my eye and watch his lips curve into a smile.

"I'm Nico. Nico Grasso."

I'm not sure what to say so I nod, acknowledging that I've heard.

"How old are you, Petal?"

It's the second time he's called me by that name and an unbidden warm sensation settles in the pit of my stomach. I attempt to shake it off.

"Why do you call me, Petal?" I turn to look at him and immediately wish I hadn't. I'm captured by the flex of his muscles beneath his black tee and fascinated by the tattoos which cover both arms and run up his neck. I force myself to turn back to the window and concentrate on the tree lined streets we are travelling down. When they open to reveal a beach, sea air filters into the car. I roll down the window and put my fingers into the breeze, the warm air lapping at them.

Something flutters in my belly and I'm unsure if I like where these feelings are taking me. I suck in a few deep breaths, close my eyes and enjoy the rocking motion of the car. The sea air mingles with the scent of the beast of a man who could prove to be my savior and I find myself dozing off.

The car slowing and the sound of tyres crunching on gravel has my eyes snapping open. It takes me a moment to realize where I am and that I'm alone with a strange man. My heart rate peaks, beads of sweat form and roll down my spine. I shudder and sink into the comfort of his warm jacket. I'm comforted when his hand reaches for mine and I turn to see the kindness in his eyes. I give him a weak smile before he steps from the car, walks around and opens my door. His body fills the small space when he leans across me to unfasten the seatbelt. The air seems to be sucked from my surroundings and the loud click of the belt in the silence causes me to jump.

Nico cocks his head to one side and studies me. "Ready, Petal?"

"Um f..for?" My nerves cause me to stutter. I blow out a light breath and shake my head to clear the bad thoughts which have invaded.

"Shower, food and an actual bed."

My mouth drops open at the mention of a real bed. He must see the shock which washes over me and mistakes it for fear.

"The spare bed, Petal." His voice has a humorous tone. "Unless you wanna sleep in mine." He winks and I feel my face heat.

Before I can respond, he slides one arm under my legs, wraps one around my back and scoops me against him. He kicks the door shut and heads through a black wrought iron gate towards a stunning white two-storey house. There are numerous glass windows and a wraparound balcony has frosted glass panels to prevent falls. Pure, utter child-like excitement fills me and I finally lose control over the butterflies I have been holding at bay. They take flight in my belly as this beast of a man carries me into his home.

He unlocks the door and pushes it open, we step into the most stunning home I've ever seen. It reminds me of the homes I used to see on the television screens, some house and garden shows I watched through electronic shop windows when I wandered the streets late at night.

I peer ahead to admire spotless white, plush carpet as he kicks the door closed behind us. I can imagine it would be like walking on air.

We pass from the small entry area into an enormous living area. It has a huge, and I mean huge, grey suede look wraparound couch. It's placed so when seated you look through a window with a view of the beach below. On the far wall is a television which takes up the entire space. Everything in the room is over-sized.

To the left is a white marble kitchen with teal colored accents. Nico continues on, up three small steps and into another room which has a large unmade bed. It has pride of place in the center and glass doors open onto a balcony overlooking the beach. He places me down on the bed before walking into an adjoining room.

"Sorry for the mess, Petal." His voice trails away. "I don't have much company."

I surprise myself by giggling, I can't remember the last time I laughed, let alone giggled. I look around at the untidy man mess and sink my fingers into the super soft sheets. The softness is blissful against my dirty, chapped skin which is stretched tight, sore, dirty and gross. I lift my hands and place them over my belly, not wanting to soil the sheets. I pick at the dirt under my broken fingernails for a few moments.

Blowing out a deep breath, I push to my feet, pad to the glass doors, place my hand on the cool metal handle, click it down and push the door open. I step out onto the balcony and the warm ocean breeze washes over me. It feels amazing, I wrap my arms around my waist.

I shouldn't be here. I shouldn't dirty his home, soil his life with me and my demons. I should leave and go back to the streets where scum like me belongs. You see, when you're told over and over you're scum, you come to believe it.

I jump when his arms wrap around me. My senses must be off, living on the streets has taught me to know when someone is sneaking up on me. Damn, he has me totally off balance.

"The bath is ready, Petal." His warm breath kisses my neck.

My head lolls back as I allow his words to wash over me. His hands gather mine and he leads me back inside to the bathroom. Hot steamy air is filled with the scent of musk and pine. Butterflies erupt in my belly for a second time.

"Everything you need is in here. I've put some clothes on the rack over there." He points to a set of shelves off to one side before continuing. "I'll be in the kitchen, Petal, cooking something to eat. Take your time and relax."

His lips caress my forehead and a smile curves my lips. When he steps off to one side of me, I catch sight of my reflection in the mirror. My face is lit up like a Christmas tree. I feel foolish as I stand there, my hair matted, face covered in grime. I drop my gaze to the floor, I feel like a bloody idiot and heat creeps over my cheeks.

"Thank you," I murmur to the ground. My voice is barely a whisper.

His fingers grip my chin and he tilts my head up, our eyes meet.

"Petal, don't hide from me. I won't hurt you."

I nod. My nerves are in overdrive, my body filled with strange feelings and chills. Being here, with him, in this room, in this place, has my body being assaulted from all directions.

"You're going to be okay, Petal. I'll heal the broken in you."

Before I have a chance to formulate a response, he leaves the room and I hear the soft click of the door as it closes. I'm left alone, surrounded by the scent of him in this small but perfect place.

I'm trying like hell to fight this, whatever *this* is. It seems like one moment in his arms causes everything from the past to disappear. How can I feel this way after everything I've been through? I promised myself I would never again allow anyone to take anything from me yet after no more than an hour of knowing this man, I would be willing to fall into his arms and trust he would catch me.

I strip out of Nico's jacket and shed my dirty, tattered clothes, dropping them onto the floor.

I move to the pristine white clawfoot bathtub and watch bubbles pop and shift in the water. I can't remember the last time I had a bath, usually I find my way to the beach and use the cold showers provided so swimmers can wash off the sand and salt.

Taking a deep breath, I lift a leg over the edge and lower the tips of my toes into the warm water. Tingles flash through me as unfamiliar warmth assaults my body. Closing my eyes, I attempt to adjust to the sensation and realize tears are flowing over my cheeks. I was so engrossed with the feel of the water I didn't know I was crying. Sucking in a deep breath, I wrap my arms around myself and step into the water. Lowering myself, I allow the warmth to consume me.

What am I doing here? Nico doesn't need my demons to stain his life like they have mine.

Chapter Three

Nico

What the fuck am I doing? The thought plays on a loop as I head to the kitchen. It seems every time I'm near her, I struggle to control myself. I've tried so hard not to touch her but when I found her standing on the balcony looking out over the water, even covered in dirt and weary tattered clothes, she was absolutely gorgeous and I couldn't resist the urge to hold her. When she lifted her head and closed her eyes, it was the first time I'd seen such peace cross her face. Everything within me wants to make sure that look is always there.

I drag my hands down my face as tiredness rakes over me. Reaching over, I flip on the radio before grabbing what I need from the fridge. *Poison* by *Alice Cooper* fills the air and gives me pause to wonder. Am I caught in her web? Will wanting her destroy what I have managed to piece back together over the past four years? I swore I would never put myself through such heartbreak again. When I lost the love of my life, it came close to breaking me. Could

I do it again? Could I allow myself to become vulnerable to another woman? Fuck, I haven't even known this girl for a few hours and I can already picture what a life with her would be like. Fuck, I need to push these feelings away, get my head back on straight. I have to concentrate on the shit which is going down in my family. Antonio was right, I have to stop thinking with my dick and start doing what needs to be done. My phone rings, breaking me out of my fucked-up head and I couldn't be more thankful for the distraction.

"Si, Antonio."

"Nico, get your ass over to Dominic's house and lock it down. Nobody goes in or out. Kat is on her way there now."

"What the fuck is happening?"

"That piece of shit – Bruno J – broke into Sergio's and grabbed Kirsty. Theo is injured and Mickey is dead. Madre stronza (motherfuckers). Just get yourself over there." I hear the anger in Antonio's voice.

"Si, Capo Bastone, I'll be there in ten."

Fuck. I click end on the call and push the phone into my pocket. I hurriedly plate up the bacon and eggs I've cooked for my Petal. Fuck, *my Petal*. I don't have time to think on this now, I need to get going.

I'm about to go in search of Josie when she appears in the doorway and hesitantly makes her way into the room. I lift my hand and grip my chest as my heart stutters at the sight before me. Holy. Fucking. Shit. She is wearing the sweats I left out and they are rolled up at the ankles and at the waist. She has them matched with one of my tees which swims on her tiny body. She looks so small and my stomach twists at the sudden possessiveness which hits me. All thoughts of leaving her alone flee, the only thing left in my head is – MINE.

"Is everything okay?" she asks.

After blowing out a deep breath, I step around the bench which is separating us. Josie takes a small step back and I squeeze my hands into fists, resisting the urge to pull her into my arms. I'm trying hard not to scare her.

"I made you something to eat." My voice is husky, I clear my throat before speaking again. "My boss was just on the phone, I have to head out."

I watch as she looks around the room before her eyes find me and she nods her understanding.

"I don't know how long I'll be but I'll be as quick as I can. Please eat and try to get some sleep."

Her eyes widen and something flashes in her eyes but it was too quick for me to catch. As much as I want to stay and find out more about her, I need to leave.

"Please stay, we'll talk when I get back." I can hear the pleading in my voice.

"Am I not allowed to leave?" I hear a hint of fear when she speaks but I also hear strength.

"I really want you to stay."

When she locks her eyes on mine, I see a million things flash across her face. I hope to God she'll be here when I get back. Turning, I swipe my keys off the bench and head towards the front door. I need to get going so I can get the job done and get back to her.

When I reach out to open the door, I hear a stool scrape the floor and figure she's taken a seat.

"I'll be here," she shouts out, reassuring me.

I want to say a hundred things to her but I can't quite find my voice. I nod to myself as relief washes over me and I push through the door.

* * *

I speed through the streets in my sleek black Audi, my reasoning for travelling so fast? The faster I get there, get the job done, the faster I can get back home and find out more about the stunning, petite little lady who's waiting for me. I picture her sitting at the bench eating the food I'd cooked for her, just like it was a normal every day happening.

Whatever is happening better be serious because I'm bone tired and aching to touch my Petal. Deep down I know I shouldn't let her in, shouldn't allow her to get close because where there is love, pain follows. It's pain I'm not ready for, I've spent the past four years fucking my way from one mindless pussy to the next in a desperate effort to rid my body of the emptiness which has plagued me since the day all good in me was killed.

But, now I've looked into those coffee rich eyes it's as if I can't let her go. There's something pulling at me, something deep in her eyes which I've seen before either in life or my dreams. I'm unsure which it is but I am sure – I need to make her mine. She is Cuore mio and I will make sure she knows, I have no intention of letting her go. I will fix the broken in her as she will fix the broken in me. She *will* be mine.

It feels like Josie is giving me a second chance at this thing called love and I will do everything I can to keep her with me. I will show her how beautiful she is and how loved she can be. Under all the grime, the dirt, the street filth, I see the real Josie. She's scared, broken and alone but now she's in my home. My space. The one place I can be Nico, the man, not Nico, the Mafia Captain. The one place I can open my heart to her.

Shit. I'm almost at my boss' home, I came here on auto pilot. I turn off the road onto the long, sweeping laneway and stop at the wrought iron gates in front of the house. I punch in the code and wait for the gates to swing open before driving through, gliding up the driveway and parking off to one side. I note Kat hasn't arrived yet but I know she won't be far away.

I climb from the car and jog up to the front door. Before I can knock, Theo swings it open, a serious look on his face.

"Fratello, good to see you're alive and kicking."

"Fuck it's good to see you, Nico. A lot of shit has happened in the past few hours and we need to get this shit nailed down. Did Antonio fill you in?" Theo runs a hand over his head and winces as I follow him inside.

"Si. It's fucked we lost Mickey. We need to finish these pricks."

Our conversation ceases when we enter the kitchen to find Brooklyn and Evie at the kitchen bench making lunch. As usual, music is blaring.

"Miss Brooklyn." I clear my throat to draw her attention. She looks up and smiles but it disappears quickly, she must note the concern on my face.

"Sweetpea, run upstairs and wash up for lunch for mumma."

"Okay." Evie jumps down off the bar stool at the kitchen bench and runs up the stairs.

Brooklyn places the knife down she was using and jams her hands on her hips. "Theo, now Nico is here will you tell me what is happening?"

"Miss Brooklyn….." I start to speak but she shakes her head, wipes her hands on a tea-towel and stomps around the bench to stand in front of us.

"It's just, Brooklyn. Now, tell me where my fiancé is and why Theo looks like something the cat dragged in."

I take a deep breath and relay everything Antonio told me on the phone. Theo then tells her why his head is wrapped up.

Brooklyn gasps and slaps her hand over her mouth, the other rests on her pregnant belly. "Oh, God." Her eyes glass over and a few tears escape and run over her cheeks.

I speak gently. "Brooklyn, we need to make sure everything is locked and secured, Katherine will be here any minute and then we can set the alarms."

"Okay. Shit. Okay." She paces the kitchen.

I need her to calm the fuck down because Dom will have both our asses if we stress Brooklyn out and something happens to his babies.

"Brooklyn, I need you to go upstairs and check on Evie. Theo and I will get everything sorted down here."

Fifteen minutes later the front door is thrown open and Katherine walks in and begins speaking on her phone, it's Antonio. "Hey, Stud. I just arrived at Brooklyn's, have you found Kirsty?" She pauses, listening before speaking again. "Oh, thank God, otherwise I would have had to kick your asses."

I try to bite back the laugh which wants to escape as she ends the call. I open my mouth to ask where they are when the front door crashes open, hits the wall and all fucking hell breaks loose. Kat screams. Theo races in, gun drawn and I pull mine from the back of my pants. We aim our guns at the men who storm in with their guns raised. Fuck. Fuck. Fuck.

29

"Don't move you pezzo di merda (piece of shit)," I growl when another man dressed in a suit walks in and smirks.

"Who the fuck are you?" Theo growls.

Before the asshole can answer, a loud, piercing cry rings out around us.

"Don't fucking move," I snarl when I hear Evie crying to her mother.

"Mumma....Nooooo....Mommy."

"Don't touch me, asshole and get your fucking hands off my daughter," Brooklyn rages.

There's more screaming before everything goes quiet for a moment. At that exact second, Katherine loses her shit and runs at one of the men holding a gun on me. Fuck, she's quick. Pulling her leg back, she kicks him in the balls but she's not fast enough and the goon swings out, punches her in the face and knocks her to the floor. Another fuckwit drags a fighting Brooklyn down the stairs and into the living room. Fuck, if there wasn't a gun pointed at my fucking head and a bleeding Katherine at my feet, I would blow the cunt's face off.

"Dom's gonna have your fucking ass...." I snarl. I lift my chin higher so the pussy holding the gun on me has to lift his arm higher. "....if you don't take your filthy hands off his woman. Right. Fucking. Now!" I shout as the man drags away a screaming Brooklyn.

"Really? Well, I guess we'll have to wait and see." His voice is laced with malice.

Plan. I need to think of a plan. Fast. My eyes lock with Theo's, he's searching them for any hints of what we can do but I come up empty. Fuck. I'm hoping to fucking God Dom and Antonio get here. And, soon. I need to come up with a way to stall because if the shooting starts, shit will go south real fast. I can't risk that happening with women in the house.

"I can see your mind ticking over." The fuckwit in the suit chuckles. I want to put a fucking bullet in his head.

"Who the fuck are you?" I demand to know.

He glares at me and tilts his head as if debating whether or not to tell me.

"Paulie DeMarko." He speaks as if he doesn't have a care in the world.

"You always attack women and children in your business?" I'm trying to figure out why his name sounds familiar. Fuck, I need a fucking moment to think.

"Sometimes it's necessary," he shrugs.

"You're a real piece of shit," Theo spits.

Before I can open my mouth and hurl abuse at the cock who's standing in front of me, the front door crashes open and an extremely pissed off Dom storms in with his gun drawn. His face is flushed with pure rage. "Brooklyn!" he shouts out as his eyes scan the area.

"Evie, baby." His voice is laced with pain and he turns his eyes on me. I nod to the lounge where the scumbag has his filthy hands wrapped around Brooklyn, a knife held at her belly. Dom flies into a rage and lunges for him as the stronzo digs the knife into her side and she whimpers.

"Back the fuck off," the asshole snaps.

Dom freezes.

"If you or your men move, I'll stab her and you can watch her bleed out."

"What the fuck do you want?" Dom snarls through gritted teeth.

I catch the reflection of Sergio in the glass doors at the side of the living room and send a prayer to the heavens. Thank fuck he's here and can see what's going on. With him here, our numbers are even with these fuckers.

"Release the woman," Dom demands.

Paulie shakes his head and laughs as he steps over to Brooklyn.

"I won't fucking say it again. Release the woman."

I hear groaning and look down at Katherine, she's beginning to come to. Antonio calls out, "Katherine, open your eyes, baby."

"You have good taste, Grasso. Such a pretty woman, it would be a shame if something was to happen to her." He runs his hand down Brooklyn's face.

"Touch her again and I will personally pull out every one of your teeth before I slit your fucking throat."

Dom is ready to end each and every one of these fuckers but Paulie laughs and waves his hand around. From the corner of my eye I see Sergio slipping through the glass doors, gun raised, pain etched on his face. Then, I remember he has a past with this fucker.

"Don't. Fucking. Touch. Her. Asshole!" Sergio speaks in a deathly low voice. Any normal person who valued their life would have run, Sergio is a mean ass fucker when he's pissed. But, this stronzo – DeMarko, laughs like a madman with a death wish.

"Let me tell you how it's going to be. You have something of mine and I obviously have someone who means a great deal to one of you." His glare is directed at all of us but it's Theo who speaks in a whisper.

"Trixie."

Paulie faces Theo and clucks his tongue. "Got it in one. You're a smart fucker. You give me my little pie and I'll give you Trixie. If you don't, I'll kill Trixie and have her body dumped on your doorstep."

What the fuck? Is this stronzo serious? He wants a trade and who the hell is Trixie?

A loud bang echoes around us and again all hell breaks loose. Bullets start flying and I unload my clip at lightning speed and hear Dom yelling for Brooklyn to get down as I reload. Bullets ricochet around the room, time passes in a blur of smoke before the shooting finally comes to an end. I watch as Paulie DeMarko tries to make a run for it with one of his piss ant goons. I take off after them but by the time I make it out front, they're already fishtailing it down the driveway and onto the fucking street.

"Fuck!" I shout and bend at the knees to catch my breath. After a moment I straighten up and head back into the house.

"He got away. The fucker got away."

"Who?" Sergio asks me.

"The asshole in charge of these goons." I wave my hand towards the three dead fuckwits lying dead on the floor.

"Paulie DeMarko," Sergio snarls.

"He's fucking dead," Dominic shouts as he walks back into the room. He's carrying a crying, shaking, very frightened Evie in his arms. She holds her arms out to Brooklyn after I help her stand.

Brooklyn steps closer and the little girl flings herself at her mother. "Mummy."

Once Evie is safe in his fiance's arms, Dom gathers them in his arms and hugs them to him before kissing Brooklyn's forehead. When he releases them, he paces the floor like a caged lion.

"He tied my daughter to a fucking bed!"

"Fanculo," I spit.

"Piece of shit."

"That cazzo is fucking dead."

The anger in all of us is palpable.

"Angel, pack a bag now," Dominic snaps.

Brooklyn nods and repositions Evie in her arms but being heavily pregnant she's struggling.

Kat gets to her feet after reassuring Antonio she's fine and sweeps Evie into her arms.

We watch as the girls head upstairs to help Brooklyn do as Dominic asked.

"Nico, I want you at Sergio's to update security. Theo, you go too, set your shit up and find something on DeMarko and your girl. We'll talk more about your girl later."

Theo and I nod in response and head for the door. All I want to do is go to my girl and hold her in my arms but, I need to get this shit done.

Dominic continues firing off instructions as we leave. "Antonio call some of the men from Sydney and get them up here, we're going to need their help..." Dom's voice trails off as we walk out the front door.

I turn to Theo. "I need to stop off at my place, I won't be long and I'll meet you at Sergio's."

"Don't take too long, Dominic will have your fucking balls if you're not there before him."

"Si fratello, I'll be ten minutes behind you."

Not wasting another minute, I jump in my car and head straight for my Petal. I need to know she's safe.

Chapter Four

Josie

By the time I finish eating, I feel full for the first time in a long time. A wave of exhaustion washes over me. I need sleep but I'm also mentally tired and today has been so intense. I find my way back to Nico's bedroom and run my fingers over the crisp covers which adorn his bed. Everything in his home is soft and plush, I worry I'm tainting it by being here.

I draw the covers back and slide between the sheets, the bed sucks me into its comfy depths. It's as if it was made especially for me as it molds to my shape. I turn onto my side facing the door so I can see when Nico returns. I drag the pillows under my head, hooking my arm under them. My eyes are drawn to the bedside table by the soft glow of the lamp and I lean closer to study the photo frame which sits upon it. The most beautiful woman I have ever seen peers back at me. My heart tightens and my chest feels heavy as I take in her perfect features. A bite of jealousy courses through me. I have no right to be jealous, I don't even know Nico, but that fact doesn't ease the feeling.

Settling my head back on the pillows, I take a few deep breaths, willing myself not to feel this way. My eyelids become heavy as sleep is not far from taking me. Snuggling into the depths of the blankets, my eyes flutter closed and darkness overtakes me. With sleep come the nightmares which I experience every night. Of what I had. What I've lost. Something which can never be replaced. I have nothing but an empty heart and pain which runs so deep, no love could ever reach it.

I unsure how long I've been sleeping when I'm startled awake. Something soft grazes my cheek. My heart misses a beat and my eyes snap open as panic washes over me. My hand darts out and flicks back the covers to strike whoever is touching me.

"Petal, it's only me."

His soft gravelly voice is reassuring as I attempt to focus my eyes in the dim light of the room. I place my hand on my chest and attempt to calm my racing heart by taking in deep breaths.

"Sorry, I panicked." My voice sounds sleepy and weak.

"Don't stress, Petal. It's to be expected." His voice is soothing, calming.

He pulls himself up from his haunches and sits on the side of the bed. I shuffle over to give him more room.

"Living on the streets makes you hyper-aware."

His hand snakes over my hip and comes to rest at the small of my back.

"You're not living on the streets anymore."

I watch as his eyes glide over my body, drinking me in. I like the feelings which form inside me, I know I shouldn't but for once in my life, I feel wanted. Desired.

"Petal, I need to tell you something but I need you to try not to freak out."

As he speaks the words, I begin thinking the worst and my mind is racing over a million things. Not trusting my voice to speak, I nod.

"I'm Nico Grasso..."

I open my mouth to remind him he has already told me his name but he raises a finger to his mouth before he continues speaking.

"I'm a member of a Mafia family and we.... Well, we kinda have a war brewing. I need to take you to a safe house where you can stay with my brother's women while I sort out our next moves with my boss and brothers."

Holy Shit. He said all that without taking a breath or batting an eyelid. I look into his eyes and see they are kind but laced with pain and worry. I watch as he runs his hand through his hair and across the back of his neck before settling it back on my hip.

"Petal?"

The nickname he has given me sets a fire burning in my belly.

"Petal."

I blink as he breaks me out of my thoughts.

"Say something," he whispers.

Without thinking about what I'm doing, I pull his head into my hands and lay the softest of kisses to his lips. Pulling back only a fraction, I speak. "Let's go then."

He moves back, his eyes wide with shock and a million emotions play across his face.

"Did you understand what I said?" He questions me as if he thinks I must be deaf.

"Yes, every word. You don't scare me half as much as being on the streets did and the feelings I have bubbling in my belly for you." My cheeks heat and something happens deep inside me as the truth of my words hit me. I can't believe I'm thinking of opening myself up to this man. Heat flushes through me with how easily it was to blurt out the words to this strange, intriguing and dangerous man.

He stands and runs his hands through his hair and down his face which looks tired and is etched with worry. I pull myself onto my knees, reach out and place my hands on his shoulders.

"It will all be okay." I try to reassure him.

His hands slide over my sides and under my armpits. A girly giggle leaves me as the cool afternoon air kisses my bare legs, I'm wearing only his t-shirt and nothing else. He pops me down and my toes flex in the softness of the carpet. His lips place a soft kiss to my forehead and one to the tip of my nose which I scrunch up.

"You are cuore mio, Petal," he breathes into the top of my head. I feel him breathe me in as his words burn into my mind.

"Let's get going." I have no idea what the words mean but his accent slides through me. I attempt to take a step back because I can't trust myself being so close to him. I don't want to say or do anything that will spoil the moment. I have to remember, my closet is full of damage, secrets and a great deal of pain. As much as I want him, I won't soil his life

***

As Nico punches in a code to gain access to Sergio's place, he'd explained earlier where we were going, I watch the way the muscles in his arms and back flex. I'm captivated by the way he drags his fingers through his dark hair and the slight tick in his jaw.

38

I'm unaware he's parked until his warm hand engulfs mine. It causes me to jump in surprise.

"Petal, we're here."

I snap out of my head and look around, taking in the gorgeous two-storey brick house with cream colored decorative pillars framing two large wooden doors.

"Wow," I gasp.

Chuckling, Nico steps from the car and comes around to open my door. As he reaches in to take my hand, the front door opens and a man's deep voice shouts out.

"Nico, what took you so fucking long? The boss will be here any minute." He stops short when I step from the car.

"Fuck, Nico, we don't have time for this shit." He throws his arms into the air and shakes his head before turning back to enter the house.

Nico squeezes my hand and when I look up at him, I see the anger in his face.

"Vaffanculo, (Fuck off) Theo," Nico growls out before the man disappears.

"I can leave," I offer.

Snapping his head back towards me, I watch as hard eyes hit mine before softening.

"You're not going anywhere." He loosens his hold on my hand before rubbing his thumb back and forth over the back.

I try to think of something other than the way his touch is affecting me. Not being able to formulate any words, I nod my head. Lifting my hand to his mouth, he places a soft kiss on it before turning and shutting the door to the car.

He places his palm to the base of my neck and a slight tremble races through me as he leads me up to the house. We climb the few steps leading to the front doors and as we approach, my palms sweat, my mouth becomes dry. I lick my lips as fear and nervousness sets in. I can't get a handle on it at all.

Today has been insane, the craziest I've ever had and that's saying something after what I've endured since the downfall of my previous life. I swallow hard when Nico's hand squeezes mine.

"Petal, I got you, okay?" His calming, accented voice soothes my nerves. "Wherever we are, know that you're mine and there is nothing anyone can do or say to change it."

The word *mine* hits something deep within me and I take a few shallow breaths to settle my racing heart. I love the thought of being his and as much as it scares me, it also excites me.

I look into his eyes and smile before blowing out a deep breath as he pushes the large wooden door open with ease.

His arm wraps around my waist, pulling me closer into his side. I wrap my arms around my body and take in my surroundings. The magnificent home has such highly polished floors you can see yourself in them. From the entrance foyer I see a beautiful carved wooden staircase. We continue on into a family room which has comfy looking brown couches. I scan the room to absorb everything I can and see three pairs of eyes staring back at me. They are all beautiful and stunning, their beauty compliments each other. And, then there's me. I push closer to Nico's side and turn into him so he is shielding me.

"Nico, finally. I was worried something had happened to you." A beautiful redhead stands from where she'd been sitting and takes a few steps towards us. She reminds me of one of those women off the retro signs of the fifties. She's stunningly beautiful, as she steps closer, I notice a small band-aid beneath one of her eyes. I assume probably to prevent a wound from bleeding.

"Nico."

The guy he'd called Theo growls and my attention is diverted towards him.

"I'm taking Josie upstairs to settle her in one of the bedrooms, it's been a big day for her. I'll be back down in a moment."

Wrapping his arm tighter around me, he turns me towards the staircase.

"The boss," Theo calls out.

Nico answered through gritted teeth. "Not now, Theo."

"Is it going to be a problem, me being here? I can look out for myself, you don't need to worry about me." I whisper so the others don't hear what I'm saying.

"As much as I should let you go, I don't think I could." He sounds tired as we both trudge up the steps.

"Why?"

We reach the top of the stairs and he leads me off to the right, towards the end of a hallway. He opens a door and ushers me into a bedroom before closing the door. I'm still waiting for him to answer but he remains quiet. We both stand, staring at each other until he nods as if he'd come to a conclusion on what to say.

"We have a lot to talk about but right now I need to get my ass back downstairs and fix some shit before the boss arrives. But, to answer your question, I don't think I could let you go because I'm a selfish prick and there's something about you which makes everything inside me insist you're mine. My heart literally hurts at the thought of letting you go."

He blows out a breath and I figure I must be doing a great impression of a goldfish. My mouth flapping open and closed, my eyes wide.

Before I can respond to what he's said, he steps before me. I place my shaking hand over his heart and close my eyes, allowing the thumping of his heart to settle through me. I open my eyes when he brushes his fingertips lightly over my cheek and stare into the silver pools of his eyes. I'm transfixed by the color and try not to blink, not wanting to miss one tiny detail.

"Why don't you lie down while I finish what I have to do. I'll come up later to fetch you. It will give you some time before I introduce you to everyone."

I relax with his words, not realizing I needed more time before meeting his family. "Sounds like a plan, thank you."

"Always, Petal."

Leaning forward he brushes his lips over my forehead before placing a kiss on the tip of my nose, it seems he likes doing this. I lick my bottom lip before drawing it between my teeth, I really want to feel his lips on mine. Before I have a chance to lift my face, inviting him to kiss me, he takes a few steps back towards the door.

"I shouldn't be long, try and get some rest." He leaves the room, closing the door.

I sit on the edge of the bed and wonder what it would be like to kiss him. To go to sleep with his taste on my tongue. I flop back on the bed and attempt to hold back the moan which wants to escape.

Damn, I need to try and get hold of myself.

Chapter Five

Nico

Heading back downstairs, I make my way towards the family room and know what's coming when I enter and find Katherine is no longer in the room.

"What the fuck Nico. Did anything I said this morning register at all with you?" Antonio yells.

"Why the fuck are you bringing your latest lay here?" Theo snaps out.

"Hold the fuck on!" I grit out, now I'm becoming pissed.

Antonio shakes his head. "No, Nico. If you want to be a man whore, fine, but right now we need your fucking head in the game not chasing around some pussy."

"She's not...." I start to set him straight but Antonio cuts me off.

"Dominic is going to be pissed as fuck, what the fuck were you thinking?"

"She is mine!" I growl. The truth of my words hit me like a sledgehammer. "Fuck, she is cuore mio."

Antonio stops dead in his tracks when he realises what I've said and Theo stands staring at me.

"Are you sure?" Antonio asks.

There is no hesitation in my answer. "Si, she is mine."

"Fuck!" Theo says.

"About fucking time, fratello." Antonio claps me on the shoulder.

"We need to update security before the boss gets here." I change the subject because thinking about Josie is making me want to say *fuck it* and head back upstairs. I can't do that, I need to get this shit sorted out.

"Camilla would be proud." A deep voice from behind me breaks into my thoughts. Spinning around, I see Dominic with sharp eyes trained on me.

"Boss."

He holds up his hand to prevent me from speaking and waves his hand around the room.

"Nico, we are family. Don't you think we noticed the struggle you've had after losing her and your child? Something like that would destroy any man, maybe now you have found someone to ease your pain."

My stomach twists as images of the day when everything was taken away from me, flash through my mind like an old movie.

"You deserve to be happy." Theo speaks softly.

I close my eyes as the next words spill from me. "I will always love Camilla, she will always have a place in my heart, but the minute I touched Josie.....It was as if the earth shifted and tilted beneath me. A feeling of peace settled in my core and I have never felt anything like it in my life."

"You found your soulmate." Brooklyn's soft voice has me opening my eyes and I notice her standing behind Dominic with her hands on her very pregnant belly.

I nod my head.

"But, you feel guilty," she adds.

I nod again and when I notice how glassy her eyes are; I look away as my heart squeezes in my chest.

"Love her the way we know you can," she says to me.

I hate the fact that tears pool behind my eyes. Brooklyn must see the guilt which lives behind my eyes.

"She would be happy you have someone to call yours again, Nico." She steps into my space; her hands raise to cup my cheeks "She would love that you have someone to call your own to love. The guilt has no place in your life and doesn't belong in your eyes."

Her words cut me deep as the truth sets in. My Camila was perfect and she would hate that I've been playing around since her death. She can finally rest knowing I have found someone who can accept my love, my secrets. Someone I can build a life with.

Brooklyn's lips find my cheek, gently kissing it. "Believe," she murmurs before biting her lip in an attempt not to laugh when Dominic growls out her name. She doesn't respond but continues speaking. "We all deserve love, Nico."

I know she's right, I grin and nod.

"Brooklyn?" Dominic grits out.

She shakes her head and shrugs at her husband's display of jealousy before turning, wrapping her arms around Dominic and whispering in his ear. She then leaves the room.

"Right, enough of this mushy bullshit. We need to get down to the matter at hand." Dom turns and heads towards the kitchen. We all follow and move to a solid oak, glossy table and chairs which stands in an area off to one side.

"I need to update the security…" I begin as we take a seat, but Theo cuts me off.

"It's done. I took care of it while I was waiting for you to turn up."

"Grazie, brother." I nod.

Shit. I run a hand through my hair, feeling like shit that I dropped the ball. I look over to where Evie lies on the floor, colouring. In the kitchen, Brooklyn and Katherine start pulling things out of cupboards and the fridge, getting organised to make dinner.

Today has kicked my ass and I hate to think I could have been the reason Dom and Antonio lost everything. Leaning my elbows on the table, I drop my head in my hands and blow out a deep breath. When I lift my head again, I notice Sergio and Kirsty aren't here.

"Where's Sergio and Kirsty?"

"Sergio took Kirsty to their room so she could have a shower they'll be down later for dinner."

"Was she hurt bad?"

"She has a few new bruises and some scrapes but that chick is badass." Antonio chuckles "The way she stabbed Bruno J – man, you do not want to get on the wrong side of her."

Before anything else is said, our attention is drawn to the doorway as Josie enters. She's shy and nervous about approaching. I jump to my feet. The chair scrapes over the polished floor, sending out a high-pitched squeal which could break glass. In a few long strides, I reach my woman's side and wrap her in my arms.

"Petal, you okay?" I ease her back slightly to look into the eyes which I now know hold my future.

"I'm fine. It's just…..um…… I was lonely up there." Her voice is barely above a mere whisper, but the women in the house hear her and Brooklyn approaches first

"I bet you were, hon." She slaps my arm in a show of disgust. "You left her up there alone, in a strange house?" The other men laugh at the way she snaps at me.

"Come on, I'll get you a hot drink and some food." She pulls at Josie's arm in an attempt to take my woman with her, but she fails. I'm not letting her go anywhere.

"Nico," Brooklyn scolds. "She'll be just over there." She points to the counter no more than half a dozen steps from us.

"I don't care," I snap and immediately regret my tone.

Josie's hands rub over my chest, her face is a rosy shade of pink with embarrassment. "It's okay, Nico. I'm not going anywhere, I'll be fine and you can see where I am."

I clear my throat, brush a few strands of hair from her face and keeping my eyes locked on hers, I introduce her to my family.

"This is Josie. She's mine now. All of her. The past, present and future."

Her mouth drops open at my declaration.

"I found her behind a skip bin at the club this morning and as soon as my eyes met hers, I knew she was the other half of my heart and soul. All her scars, secrets from the past, will not turn me away from loving her. I ask you to take her as your family as you have me."

I speak to them all before focusing on Josie when I see the doubt which lives behind her eyes. "Petal, it doesn't matter how dark your past is or what made you take to the streets, I will love you."

Tears slide from her rich, beautiful hazel eyes and I wipe them away with the pad of my thumb before dropping my mouth to hers and kissing her softly in front of my family. Cementing it in stone, showing them and especially her, that she is mine.

"Nico, you don't know what you are getting yourself into with me," she chokes out.

"I don't care. I want you and I will accept everything that comes with you."

"You don't even know me."

"Tell me you felt it," I urge.

"Felt it?" Her eyebrows draw in.

"The first time I touched you, I felt it to my bones. A sensation like nothing I have ever felt before. My whole body vibrated with that one touch."

Fuck, I sound like a fucking pussy, but I need to know she feels it too.

"I'm addicted to you, Josie. It's as if I'm a fucking drug addict and the only thing that can settle this fucking craving is you. So, I'm asking. Do you feel it too?" I hold my breath as I watch a million emotions flash across her face before she sucks her bottom lip into her mouth.

"This is crazy. I haven't even known you a day, but yes, I feel it. I crave everything that is you."

A smile kisses her lips and I find myself needing another taste. Leaning down I run my tongue across her bottom lip, causing a small gasp to escape and taking the opportunity, I slip my tongue into her mouth. I take control as I feel her control slip, her taste consumes me. Running one hand through her hair, I hold her tight, needing more.

"Nico, brother." A hand lands on my shoulder and I pull back from my woman's mouth. "We have shit to do, so pull up your big girl panties and let's get down to business. You can taste your woman later." Antonio chuckles.

"Fuck off," I growl

"Stud, leave them alone. That was one of the sweetest things I've ever seen," Katherine calls out from the kitchen.

"Sweet?" I growl which causes Josie to laugh. It's such a beautiful sound and warms my chest.

"Petal, go to the kitchen while we try and sort some shit out before I take your ass upstairs and show you how fucking sweet I can be."

I feel the tremble run through her. She bites her lip and gazes up at me through her eyelashes. I have to bite back a groan at the sight. Fuck, my Petal is sexy as fuck and I can't wait to get her alone. Turning her towards the kitchen and a smiling Brooklyn, I swat her ass lightly before returning to the table. I take the opportunity to adjust myself as I go because I'm hard as fuck.

"Antonio, I need you to go and grab the bag from the car, the one we took from the house earlier," Dominic says.

"What did you find?" Theo asks as he opens his laptop.

"We found a room at the back of the house Kirsty was located in. It had a couple of computer monitors, a bed and a small bar fridge."

"Shit," Theo growls

Dominic blows out a deep breath before he goes on. "It looked like there had been a struggle."

"Fuck, Boss we need to find her." Theo's fingers fly over the keys of his keyboard.

"Antonio and I found a few portable hard drives and USB sticks under the mattress of the bed and I also found this....." Reaching into his pocket, he pulls out a folded piece of paper and hands it over to Theo. As he unfolds it, a photo falls out and lands face down on the table. Theo reads what's on the paper.

"It's a birth certificate for someone called, Trinity Hope." He picks up the photo studies it. "Holy fucking shit." His eyes are transfixed on the picture. "We need to find her, Boss."

"So, it's her?" Dom asks.

"I feel it in my bones, it's my Trixie." He continues staring at the photo.

Antonio places the bag he's retrieved from the car, onto the table.

"We need to get a plan together and find this son of a bitch and we need to make sure the woman stay protected at all times. I called Johnny and he's calling up some of our soldiers, they should be here in the next 48 hours. Until then, we need to work out where this motherfucker is," Antonio snaps.

"Hand me the bag, I'll see what's on the hard drives and USB sticks. Fingers crossed, my Trixie will have left me a trail to find them." I can hear in Theo's voice just how worried he is.

"Si, get on it. Nico you look like you haven't slept in days, try and get some rest. If we find anything, we'll wake you up."

"Boss...." I begin to protest, but Dominic holds his hand up, stopping me.

"It wasn't a request, Nico. I need you to get on your game and have your head on fucking straight. I do not want a fucking repeat of today, do you understand me?"

"Si, Boss." I nod and get to my feet. There's no point arguing, I know I fucked up today so it's best if I walk away now.

"Take Josie with you." He nods towards her and I can see how tired she is.

I nod, cross the room, take her hand and without saying a word, I lead us towards the stairs and up to our bedroom for the night.

Chapter Six

Josie

As I enter the bedroom with Nico, I know the time has come to open up and tell him how dark my past is. Running my finger over my tingling bottom lip, I can still feel the kiss. It was magic, sensual, owning and meant just for me.

"Petal, what's worrying you?" Nico's voice is laced with tiredness and he flops down on the bed. He rests his head and torso against the black leather headboard, his long legs stretched out over the scarlet red cover. He pats the bed, wanting me to sit down. I move closer and he lifts me between his legs. My head falls back against his chiseled chest. Amazing feelings wash over me as he runs his hands over my shoulders and collarbones. I close my eyes and bathe in the gentleness of his touch.

"Petal, tell me all about the mystery of Josie."

His voice vibrates from his chest into me, sending chills to the very center of my heart and bouncing around like a ball in a pinball machine. My nerves go on alert and dread settles deep in my belly. I know I have to be honest with him and I know it sounds foolish, but I'm terrified of losing him when he finds out about me.

I draw in a deep breath and blow it out slowly. Then, I decide to lay my soul bare and hope he can shoulder what I say. I wiggle deeper against him, his hands fold over my belly.

"I need to tell you everything at once."

"Petal, I'm listening." His voice sends chills dancing down my spine.

"When I was sixteen, I got pregnant to my first ever boyfriend. I had no idea what I was going to do. He was older than me at nineteen and my mother hadn't approved of him. When I told her I was pregnant, she lost it and kicked me out. I walked all the way into town to where my boyfriend lived. He was shocked and mad but took me in anyway. We began planning for the arrival of our baby. It was a baby boy and not long after he was born, I found out he'd been cheating on me the entire time we'd been together."

I paused and took another deep breath.

"I was upset and angry, he'd said he loved me and yet had someone on the side. He insisted he loved us, wanted us and said he'd tell her it was finished. He didn't, all he wanted was for me to do the cooking, cleaning and laundry while he had his bit on the side. The weekend trips and late nights suddenly made sense. I packed a bag and was getting ready to take our son and leave him. He caught me doing it, exploded and I copped a beating. He took our son and left. I haven't seen or heard from him since. A short time later, I was kicked out of the apartment when I couldn't pay the rent. So, it was the streets. I had nowhere to go. I did what I had to, to survive. Rummaged through bins behind café's and restaurants. Stole from stores when the owner wasn't watching. Then, you found me when I was searching through the skip for something to eat and now I'm here. I miss my son so much, my heart aches for him."

I blew out a huge breath, it felt good getting my past out in the open. Nico's silence is deafening and I turn in his arms to see his face is damp with tears. A combination of shock, pain and loss haunted his eyes. I placed my hands to the sides of his face, forcing him to look at me.

"Babe, are you okay? I'm sorry, I understand if you want me to leave." I close my eyes and pull back from him, his hands snap around my wrists.

"Petal, I *never* want you to leave." He takes a deep breath and wipes the tears from his face. "I need to tell you something about me."

I nod for him to continue.

"I had a beautiful woman who I loved with all I am. She was carrying my baby and I was the happiest man alive. Then, four years ago, my entire world crashed down around me. She died during childbirth and our baby didn't survive. So, Petal, I know your pain. I feel it every day and I vow to you now, I will return your son to you, his mother, where he belongs."

His voice is low, harsh with a clip to it which sends goosebumps over my skin. For the first time since my nightmare began, I feel myself waking up and hope that I may get my son back.

"He turned six almost a month ago. I've missed so much time with him, Nico."

"How long has he been gone?"

"Two years. He probably wouldn't even know who I am."

"What's his name?"

"Joseph."

"That's a strong boy's name, Petal."

I turn in his arms and straddle his thighs, place my hands to the sides of his face and peer deep into the eyes which hold so much.

"Were you serious when you said I was yours?"

His hands rest on my hips and his thumbs circle my hip bones.

"Yes, I was and I'm yours."

"Mine," I whisper, testing the word on my tongue. I love the way it rolls in my mouth.

"Always, Petal."

"When we were downstairs, you said you loved me....."

His lips crash against mine. I allow him to take control as a myriad of emotions run through me. I can't seem to get enough of this man. I'm addicted to his taste, the way his scent assaults my senses and I don't want to ever let go. He pulls back and rests his forehead against mine and what he says next, blows my mind.

"I love you, like I've never loved anyone in my life."

I see the truth in his eyes as he speaks and sparks shoot through me when I realize, I love him too.

"I love you, too." I manage to whisper before his lips caress mine.

I run my hands through his hair as I rock back and forth on his lap, his hardness pressing against my ass. Pulling back, I rest my forehead against his.

"Fuck you taste good, Petal." Nico runs his hands over my sides causing goosebumps to break out over my body.

I'm not sure how to ask for what I want so, I reach down and start sliding his shirt up his body until he takes over and pulls it over his head. I slide my hands over every ripple of his hard chest.

My mouth waters at the sight of his body covered in tattoos. *Fuck my man is sexy*. I stifle a giggle by pulling my bottom lip between my teeth.

I feel my shirt being eased up and lock eyes with him as he slowly peels it from my body. Embarrassment engulfs me, heat creeps over my cheeks and I lower my head, allowing my long hair to fall in waves over me. I keep my eyes on his chest as he draws the shirt over my head. I feel the warmth of his hand when he slides it under my chin and lifts my face up to his.

"Don't hide from me, Petal. You are sexy as fuck." He runs a finger across my bottom lip, freeing it from my teeth.

Keeping his eyes locked on mine, he slides his rough hands down my back. I tremble and my head lolls back, a moan slips from my lips. Arousal is taking over, my senses are being over-run by his delicious touch and the sensual feelings Nico evokes in me.

He rolls me to the side so I'm now beneath his shirtless body. An animal need in me wants to tear the shorts from his body but I lie patiently while he rakes his eyes over my body before returning to my face.

"You're stunning, Petal." His voice is gruff with sex laced need.

My face burns as I stare into his eyes. His hands find my sides, his cool fingertips grazing along my rib cage and down to my hips. I suck in a deep lungful of air as I buck my hips from the bed. His touch is slow, agonizingly sensual. I can barely contain myself.

Nico chuckles. "Eager, my Petal?"

I open my eyes to watch him hook his fingers in the waistband of my sweats and in one uber slow movement, he eases them down. I lift my bum, allowing him to pull them all the way down. He tosses them over his shoulder and onto the floor.

"That's better, my Petal."

He stands at the side of the bed and begins to strip off his shorts. The angel in my mind tells me to turn away. The devil in me says, *"fuck no, bask in this god who is all yours now, sweetheart."* And, that's what I do. The heat rushes into my cheeks when the size of his throbbing cock is revealed. I panic slightly wondering how I will ever take him inside me.

I've only ever been with one man and he wasn't anywhere near as massive as this man. My eyes must be wide, full of shock because Nico laughs as he crawls up the bed to rest over my body. His heat chasing away the chill which has overcome me.

"Don't worry, Petal. I promise you, it will fit and I'll take it slow and gentle."

"Okay." My voice is shaky and it's all I manage to get out.

He lowers his body onto me and his lips seek out mine in a kiss which is filled with primal need. Our tongues twist and tangle like they had always meant to meet. Sparks fly, the air crackles around us, my hands move over his thick, muscular back. Fingernails scrape at his flesh, over his shoulders and he groans into my mouth before breaking the kiss.

"I can't wait too much longer, Petal." His voice is needy, filled with desire and want.

"Well, don't." I shock myself with my forwardness.

When he slides his hand down my side, I arch into his touch, feeling every hard ridge as my body presses against his. He cups the back of my knee and lifts it until it lays across his lower back. I feel the hardness of his cock press against my pussy. When he slides his fingers through the wetness, I moan, needing much more.

"So fucking wet for me." He pushes one finger, then two, inside me.

I moan and dig my nails into his shoulders causing him to hiss.

"Need you now." He removes his fingers and slides the head of his cock across my aching clit.

"I'm going in bare, babe. You're mine. There will be no-one else." He groans as he pushes into me.

I yelp slightly but arch into him as he slides deeper. Absorbing all of him as he pushes against my tight walls, stretching me. There is a feeling of fullness and absolute bliss. Wrapping my legs over his back, I lock my ankles together and urge him in further. Using my feet against his back, I guide him back and forth. In and out. I need more. No, I want more. I want everything he has to give.

His eyes meet mine and a wild hunger flashes through them. What little is left of my self-control is lost and what's happening between us takes over. We grind together in one fluid movement like we've been fucking each other forever.

I feel the heat of his balls slapping against me. My nails bite into his flesh and he rears back on a hiss, locking his eyes on mine. Concern almost fear flashes in them.

"I'm okay," I pant. "Lose control, babe."

The look in his eyes is replaced by need which must be mirrored in mine.

His head falls back onto his shoulders and the vein in his neck pulses with his intense heart rate. My hand rests on his chest.

His fingers dig into the bones of my hips as he lifts my ass from the bed and thrusts into me, hard and deep. I can't control the scream which leaves me, a grunt of satisfaction leaves Nico and I feel the apex of our joint arousal forming. Speeding up from the very depths of our bodies. He thrusts faster, in and out. Sweat licking our skin. His rhythm becomes erratic and I lock my legs tighter around his waist to hang on.

"Take me, Nico. Make me come for you." I plead with him on a deep moan.

As I start to buck to meet his thrusts, his hand moves between us, capturing my aching clit between his finger and thumb. I lose all control, coming hard as he also lets go. Exploding around me, my name leaves his lips and echoes around us. Ripples of ecstasy wash over me, triggering a second orgasm I think will never end.

Breathless and craving his taste, I pull his head down to me and take his mouth hard and fast. My throbbing, wet pussy remains needy, wanting more.

His chest rests against me, his weight pushing us deeper into the mattress. My hands rest on his clenched ass cheeks. We remain silent, attempting to catch our breath. I enjoy the ripples and aftershocks of the hungriest, neediest, unforgiving sex I have ever experienced.

"Mine," he growls on a deep exhale.

"Yours. Always yours, mio Santo."

He draws in a sharp breath when I call him my saint in Italian.

Chapter Seven

Nico

Burying my nose into my woman's hair, I take a deep breath of her scent, letting it work its way through me. I kiss her temple and watch her as she sleeps. The way her thick eyelashes rest against her porcelain white cheeks, how her bow shaped lips part when she breathes in and out. I thank God for giving me this second chance. I kiss her temple one more time before pushing myself from the bed. I need to call Johnny and get this shit sorted.

I throw a pair of shorts on and take one last look at Petal before closing the door with a soft click. I pad down the stairs and find Antonio and Theo deep in conversation at the kitchen table. I give them a chin lift before moving to the fridge and grabbing a jug of water. I grab a glass from the cupboard beside the fridge.

While pouring, I ask, "Have you spoken with Johnny tonight, Antonio?"

"Si, a little earlier."

"I need to call him. Did he say if he was busy tonight?" I glance at the time on the microwave to see it's just after 9pm.

"He didn't say but I don't think so. Why? What's up, fratello?"

Shit. Fuck. I debate about whether or not to tell them but if I don't, they are bound to find out sooner or later. I take a seat at the table and lay it all out for them. I watch my fingers rubbing at the condensation on the glass as I speak. I tell them how Josie's son of a bitch boyfriend cheated on her, beat her up, took her son and left her homeless. When I look up, it's too stare into two pairs of very pissed off eyes.

"Piece of shit!" Theo rages.

Antonio slams his fist down hard on the table. "Call Johnny, get this shit sorted and get your boy back where he belongs."

I grab the phone from my pocket, pull up Johnny's number and as my finger hovers over the call button, Antonio's words repeat inside my head.

"*My* boy?" I feel like I can't catch my breath. *My boy.* I work hard to get my head around the words.

Antonio nods. "Josie is your woman, is she not?"

"Fuck. I need to get my boy back."

"How the fuck are you going to find him? Do you have any idea of where he might be?" Theo asks.

"Josie and I talked before she fell asleep, she told me the asshole's name. The apartment they lived in was in his name. It's not much, but it's something."

"That's a start," Antonio agrees.

I pick up my phone from the table and hit *send* on Johnny's number. He answers on the third ring.

"Nico." His voice is crisp and low.

"Johnny."

"What's up?"

"I need someone found and fast."

I hear him moving about on the other end of the phone. The scraping of chair legs is loud and I assume he is headed for his office.

"Are you busy?"

"Never for my famiglia."

I let out the breath I hadn't realised I'd been holding. I really need his help to get this shit sorted.

"Thanks, fratello. His name is Dan Reynolds and his last known address is 10 Wells Street Adamstown in New South Wales. He has a kid with him. A boy, aged six. He beat my woman, took my kid and did a runner, leaving her at the mercy of assholes on the streets. I want him found. Now!" Venom laces my voice, my knuckles turn white and I feel the tic in my jaw.

"Figlio di puttana," he hisses. "I'm on it, give me thirty minutes."

"Grazie, fratello." I blow out a deep breath and disconnect the call.

"Well?"

Dom's deep voice startles me and when I turn, his eyebrow is raised. I was too focused on the call to notice both he and Sergio had returned to the kitchen.

"Thirty minutes. I need to call him back in thirty minutes." I can feel the tension rolling off me in waves, push up from the table and begin to pace the length of the kitchen. Waiting has never been my strong suit and now time seems to be passing at a snail's pace.

Dom moves over to me and hands me a beer. "Calm down. Try to relax."

"Fuck, calming down," I snap and immediately regret it when his hand clamps down on my shoulder and squeezes hard.

"It will work out."

I stare through the kitchen window, waiting for the thirty minutes to pass, it's painfully slow. I lift the beer to my lips but before I can swallow, I hear my phone vibrate where I left it on the table. Sergio picks it up and hands it to me as I rush over.

"Johnny, what have you found out?"

"It's good and bad news,"

I clench my jaw and feel the pop under the strain.

"He's dead. The asshole died in a car crash. He was driving drunk and wrapped his car around a tree. That's the good news."

"The bad?" My stomach is turning somersaults.

"The kid has been placed in State care. He's been in and out of foster homes, shifted here and there. At the moment he's in a home for boy's not far from you guys."

Relief floods me. "Thanks, Johnny. Text me the address. I'm gonna go and get my boy and bring him home." Tears choke my voice. I disconnect the call and shove the phone in my pocket. I turn to the other men in the kitchen. "You coming, guys?"

They stare at me, shock clear on their faces.

"What?" I snap. I don't have time for this shit.

The phone pings in my pocket, indicating an incoming text. I pull it out and note the address is only ten minutes away. I grab my keys off the counter and head towards the door.

***

63

Street lights flash by in a blur as I drive down the road. Sergio and Dom haven't uttered a word since we left the house. I find the address and pull into a driveway beside a sign which reads – 'Home for the Unwanted.' Holy fuck. My boy isn't unwanted. This breaks my fucking heart. I shift the car into park, switch off the engine and reach into the glove compartment for an envelope of money. We all exit the car and a beep sounds in the night when I push a button the remote to lock up.

We head for the front door, carefully negotiating a bunch of broken steps. The place is dimly lit and run down. I push the intercom button and I'm surprised it actually works. A woman's voice comes through loud and clear.

"Can I help you? It's quite late."

"I'm here for Joseph Stenson," I reply.

"Oh, I see. Are you a relative?"

"Yes." I struggle to keep my voice even, knowing there isn't a chance in hell she'll open the door if she feels threatened.

A buzzer sounds, I push the door open and we step inside. A rush of cold air hits me. This place is fucking terrible. Looking ahead, I see the woman I've been speaking to. She's short, a little round in the middle with gray hair. She walks down a hallway to greet us.

"Gentlemen, my name is Stella." She shakes our hands before speaking again. "I don't usually receive visitor's this late at night. You know Joseph? You said you were family?"

None of us misses her perusal of us and she has a puzzled expression on her face.

"His mother is my partner. We've been searching for him for quite a while. His father took him without permission. We received word he was here about half an hour ago and we're here

64

to take him home." My voice has become clipped and she indicates for us to follow her.

We're led down a hallway to a small room which holds far too many sleeping boys. We weave through the beds to a trundle bed in the far corner.

"This is your little boy," she whispers.

I step forward and set eyes on my little boy for the first time, it won't be the last. I lean over and scoop him into my arms. He stirs a little and not wanting to frighten him, I run my hand soothingly over his back until his head comes to rest on my chest. "I'm taking you home, little man," I whisper. He hums in response before saying a sleepy, "Okay."

Stella has her arms folded across her chest as she watches us. "I shouldn't let you take him until child services approves it, but if this sweet boy has a chance at a good home, and I know in my heart he does with you then, I'm making an executive decision and allowing you to take him. He doesn't belong in here." Her voice is full of compassion.

I reach into my pocket, withdraw the envelope and hold it out to her. "This has cash in it, get some repairs done and whatever else you need for these kids."

Her kind eyes glass over with tears as she takes it from my hand. "I need some basic information from you before you leave."

We follow her to an office and I don't hesitate to give her the information she requires.

"Thank you," she murmurs when we're done.

We leave the office and head for the front door where Dom and Sergio have been waiting for me. I throw the car keys to Sergio, indicating I want him to drive.

When we reach my car, Dom opens the back door and I slide onto the seat with a still sleeping Joseph in my arms. While Sergio negotiates his way back to the house, I stare at my boy's little face in the glow of the street lights. His features are so small, so perfect. I'm transfixed by his perfection and don't realise we have arrived back at Sergio's until he switches off the engine and Dom speaks.

"Nico, get him settled into bed, tomorrow will be a big day and I know Brooklyn and Evie are going to insist on meeting him."

"Si, Boss, and thank you."

Dom waves my thanks away. "It's what family does for each other. Just make sure it's what you want and you're not going to fuck around on Josie and this little boy. They've both been through more than enough."

"They're my world, Boss. Everything I've always wanted, needed. Josie is cuore mio."

"Si, brother. If she truly is your heart as you say, you have my blessing."

I feel a lump form in my throat as emotion overwhelms me. I know now, everything in my life has led me to this point. For now, I need to get my little man up to bed and make sure Josie is okay because this is going to blow her mind.

Dom rounds the car and opens the door for me and I slide out, careful not to disturb my son. I head into the house and cross straight to the staircase. I take the steps carefully, pass through the hallway and into the bedroom where Josie is still sleeping peacefully. I lay Joseph beside her, kneel on the floor beside the bed and run my fingers over her flushed cheek.

"Josie." I whisper so as not too wake our son. "Petal, I need you to wake up." I speak a little louder and her eyes flutter open. A smile kisses her perfect lips. "Hey, Petal." I speak quietly even though I think my kid could sleep through a bomb going off.

"Hey," she breathes out, her eyes heavy with sleep.

"Baby, I have something for you." I cup her warm cheek in the palm of my hand. "I need you to promise not to scream."

Her eyes are locked on mine as she nods.

"Look beside you, baby."

I see the moment she realises it's our son. Her eyes widen, her face pales and she begins shaking. She lifts her eyes back to mine and places a hand to my cheek.

"Really? It's him? Really?" Her lips tremble and tears roll down her cheeks.

"Yes, it's your son, Petal. I promised you I would bring him back."

She leans across her sleeping son, one hand on his chest and kisses me. The effect and memory of the last time our lips locked, flood back and my cock twitches. Now isn't the time. I break the kiss, move to the other side of the bed and slide under the covers. I wrap Petal in my arms while she wraps hers around Joseph. *Our* son, I remind myself. My little family.

"Thank you, Nico. You truly are my saint. My saving grace. You have given me back my world and I hope you want us like this, as a family."

"I want nothing more than to claim both you and Joseph as mine."

Leaning back, she turns her head and plants a soft kiss on my lips. Before pulling away, she whispers, "I love you" into my mouth.

Her words soak into every pore of my body. "I love you too, Petal. You and our boy. You're my world and I will protect you for the rest of my life."

"Thank you, Nico." Josie sniffs back her tears of joy.

"Always, Petal. Mine."

We lay in peaceful silence for a while until I feel sleep beginning to take me. But, Josie's next words have me wide awake again.

"What if he doesn't remember me?"

I hear the heartbreak, the fear and sadness in her voice and it squeezes my chest.

"Then, you will remind him every single day of his life from now on." I run my hand up and down her side until her breathing eases and I know she's asleep. For the first time in a very long time, I fall into a peaceful sleep beside her.

Chapter Eight

Josie

I'm pretty sure I only slept in half hour intervals last night. Having my little boy back in my arms seemed like a dream. I was terrified if I dropped off to sleep, I'd wake up back on the streets and everything would be gone. Instead, I lay in Nico's arms, staring at Joseph.

I run the tips of my fingers through his dark hair as tears roll over my cheeks. He looks exactly like the last time I saw him, but he's bigger. I can see the slight dip in his chin where a dimple appears when he smiles and a tiny scar on his chin from a fall as a toddler.

The sun creeps into the room and soft rays of light signal not only a new day, but the first day of the rest of my new life. A new life with my family. My son. My man. I can hardly believe Nico has done this for us and he made everything happen so quickly. I'll have to ask him how he managed everything in such a short amount of time, but for now, I'm content lying here watching the sun's rays dance over Joseph's features.

My son begins to stir, my heart stutters as he stretches his small body and soft moans come from his mouth. My hand rests on his belly and I watch as his eyes flutter open. His eyes dart around the room and shock washes over his angel-like features. I hold my breath when he turns towards me. His big brown eyes, a mirror of me, meet mine. He takes my breath away. He blinks and blinks again. Before I can utter a word, his face breaks out with a huge smile which lights up his eyes. Then I hear the sweetest word I've ever heard.

"Mummy."

His tiny, uncertain voice causes tears to pour down my face. I let out a long breath when the fear of him not knowing me, washes away.

"Mummy, it's you." He sits up and I do the same.

I hold his face gently in my hands.

"Yes. Yes, Joseph. It's me." I sniffle back a sob.

"I knew you would come, mummy. I knew it."

His hands fly around me and his head rests on my chest, right where it belongs.

"How did you know it was me?" I ask as he wriggles free.

"This, mumma." He pulls a small, tattered and bent photo from the pocket of his track pants and thrusts it into my hands. "It's a picture of me and my mummy, you and me. I took it when daddy took me away from you."

My heart breaks at the memory and sobs wrack my body.

"Don't cry, mummy. It's okay now. I'm okay." He attempts to reassure me, his voice full of wisdom beyond his age.

"I never stopped thinking about you or looking for you." I push the stray hairs from his face, kiss his forehead and wrap him in my arms, holding him close against my body.

Nico sits and wraps his arms around us both.

"Morning, family." His voice is husky with sleep.

My eyes meet his. "Morning."

"Hey, champ." He ruffles Joseph's hair and our son looks up and smiles.

"You saved me. I saw you in my dream, you said you were taking me home."

"I sure did, little guy and your mumma saved me."

Now I really am a mess of tears.

"Shall we head down and have some breakfast, champ?" Nico asks Joseph.

"Will you be my daddy now my bad daddy died? I don't want to go back to that home with the other boys."

My heart breaks for my little man and I hug him tight. "Oh, baby. My sweet baby boy. You'll never go back, your home is here now with me and Nico." I lift him up and place him between Nico and I.

"I'd be honored to be your daddy, but it's completely up to you." Nico wraps his arm around both of us and settles his hand on my waist.

"Would you ever take me away from mummy?" He places one of his tiny hands in mine and I feel him trembling.

"Never," Nico vows.

"Would you hurt us?" His voice is soft.

My heart shatters in my chest with the pain of his memory, of his daddy beating me.

"You have my word, I will never lay a hand on you or your mumma. You will come to realise, a man is only as good as his word. A man who breaks his word, is nothing."

Something eases inside me at Nico's words, I didn't know it was what I'd needed to hear. I place my hand around his waist and squeeze. As I look down at Joseph, sadness engulfs me. I have missed so much time with him, I should have done more to find him.

His gorgeous brown eyes look up at me. "Mummy, I'm hungry."

"Okay, baby. How about we go and get you fed?"

I climb from the bed to see a neatly folded pile of clothes on a chair in the corner of the room. I glance back at Nico.

"Brooklyn lent you some clothes until we can get to the shops."

Feeling as if I'm about to start crying again at her kindness, I simply nod my thanks. I pick them up before I head for a shower while Nico takes Joseph's hand and heads for the door.

"Take your time, Petal. I'll take Joseph downstairs and get started on breakfast."

"I won't be long," I assure him. I don't want to be apart from Joseph any longer than necessary, I've already lost so much time with him.

***

I hear laughter coming from the kitchen as I make my way downstairs and head towards there. As I approach the door, I hear music as a new song begins. A smile curves my lips when I hear the lyrics. I couldn't think of a better song to start a new day in our new life – *Fresh Eyes* by *Andy Grammer*. Fresh eyes indeed. I'm looking at my new life with fresh eyes and a rather full heart.

72

The whole of Nico's family is in the kitchen and it's buzzing with chatter and love. I search the room for Joseph and find him playing on the floor with a little girl. Nico is seated on a chair beside him. I walk to my man and slide my hands over his shoulders. He reaches up, grabs my hips and pulls me onto his lap. I melt into him like snow in rain.

Reaching down, I run the tips of my fingers through Joseph's hair, he looks up at me and a smile brightens his face. I smile back and whisper, "I love you."

He whispers back, "I love you too, mummy."

My heart swells with love and a chill rips through my body when Nico's lips tease the base of my neck.

"Petal, are you okay?"

I turn in his arms and cup his face in my hands.

"Better than okay. Happy isn't a strong enough word to explain how I feel. You have given me so much more than I could ever give you." I lower my lips to his as two little disgusted voices voice their opinions.

"Yucky," the little girl says.

"Gross, cover your eyes, Evie."

Nico breaks away from my lips, chuckling at their comments. "Hey, champ, can't I kiss a beautiful lady?

Everyone in the room bursts into laughter when Joseph declares, "Nope, not in front of Evie."

Nico leans forward, scoops him up and places him on his lap. He wraps us both in his strong arms.

"Home, my family is home," he breathes into my ear. I'm sure my heart is about to explode.

Joseph stills in our arms and when I look up, I find two new sets of eyes on us. One is a stunningly beautiful woman, the other is a huge man.

"Daddy, who are they?" Joseph turns to Nico while pointing towards the couple.

Hot tears race down my cheeks. Nico glances at me before answering Joseph.

"Well, son. They're family. Sergio is one of my brothers and the beautiful lady is Kirsty, his girlfriend."

Nico's eyes meet mine. "He called me daddy," he whispers over Joseph's head.

I can only nod, afraid if I attempt to talk, nothing would come out.

Nico gets to his feet and places Joseph down on the floor in front of him. He wraps an arm around my waist.

"Sergio, Kirsty, this is my woman, Josie. This little man, is my son, Joseph." Nico smiles wide and my heart flutters in my chest on hearing the pride in his voice.

Sergio moves a few steps closer. I watch as Kirsty looks to the ground for a moment before following a couple of steps behind. I'm worried we might not be welcomed but when I glance at Nico, he shakes his head slightly.

"Nice to meet you, Josie, Joseph." His speech is strongly accented like Nico's. He holds his hand out too shake mine and does the same with our son.

"Sugar," he calls over his shoulder.

She moves to his side and Sergio wraps his arms around her before whispering in her ear.

"I hope we aren't over-stepping by being in your home." I'm beginning to worry that we shouldn't be here.

"Oh, no. Please don't take my silence as not wanting you here. It's just....um.....I'm not used to meeting new people." She gives me a timid smile.

I know how she feels and blow out a small breath of relief.

I watch as Kirsty drops her eyes to Joseph before crouching down to be at eye level with him. She holds her hand out to him.

"It's so nice to meet you, Joseph. I see Evie has you coloring."

"Yes. I haven't colored for such a long time." He smiles and bounces on his toes a little. "Dad said he'd buy me coloring books of my own. Some with trucks and stuff instead of princesses and fairies."

I bite my lip in an attempt not to laugh at the expression on his face. I can't hold it back though when everyone else starts to laugh.

I look over to where Brooklyn and Katherine are busy with breakfast. Dom and Antonio are seated at the table watching everything that's going on. I'm in the process of wondering where Theo is when he strides into the kitchen, a laptop open in his hands. He has a worried expression on his face. I'm not sure what is wrong but I do know there is something serious happening. I resolve to ask Nico about it later when we're alone.

I glance around the room and feel the love that surrounds us. I'm so thankful Nico found me and brought me into his family. I turn to offer the girls my help when I see Kat slap her hand over her face and turn seven shades of green before she bolts from the room.

"Kitten!" Antonio springs to his feet and starts after her just as a buzzer sounds.

"Front gate," Sergio calls out.

I notice Dominic glance at Brooklyn and it's as if they have a silent conversation between them. She nods and wipes her hand on a tea-towel before moving over to us and the kids.

"How about we take the kids outside and they can play. Kirsty, maybe you can show Joseph how to make a wish on a dandelion." Brooklyn smiles at me.

I look to Nico who nods for me to go ahead

"Sure, sounds good." I help the kids up from the floor and follow them outside.

After about twenty minutes, I offer to grab cold drinks from the fridge. When I reach the kitchen, I hear the clipped and sharp voices of the men as they speak.

"Sorry, I didn't want to interrupt." I feel my cheeks heat when all eyes fix on me.

"It's okay, Petal," Nico reassures.

I reach for the drinks in the fridge and when I glance over at the table, I note Theo's laptop is open and all the men are watching the screen. When it pings and lights up, I see the dark image of a stunning woman in a room which is completely bare of furniture. Her eyes are red from crying and her mouth is taped shut. Codes and words flash across the screen in some sort of hidden message. A man beside her is demanding, scary as hell and his cold killer eyes stare at us.

"Fuck, we need to find where she is." Anger wafts off Theo. "I can't crack the codes I know she's putting in the messages he's making her send. I know she would be infiltrating the codes with clues of where she is and how to get her."

I sense his pain. I feel it in my heart and it hurts. The screen turns black and he bangs his fist on the table. It sends out a loud crack through the room, causing me to jump and I let out a yelp. The men's eyes fall on me, Theo's are laced with anger and pain.

"Fuck, I'm sorry," Theo says.

Nico crosses to me and wraps his arms around my shoulders. "I'm okay. Let me take a look."

I move closer to the table, pull out a chair and sit down. The heat from their stares is intense and I know I need to explain.

"I know computers, I used to be a programmer." My voice is full of confidence I really don't feel. It's been a long time since I've done anything like this.

Theo slides the laptop across. "We'll take all the help we can get right now, Josie. I'm at the top of my game, doll, but hopefully you might see something I've missed." His voice sounds almost mocking as I scroll through the codes and messages.

"A fresh pair of eyes never hurts." I watch the green codes flick past in front of my eyes and follow them down while I scribble on a piece of paper beside me. The room is silent apart from the men's anxious breathing and my own thumping heart which I'm sure they can hear.

It seems like forever before I find it all, woven in between the death threats and the, *I'll beat her black and blue, I'll wipe her memory and ruin her looks so no man would ever look at her.* Jeez this guy is something else but I find what I'm looking for buried deep in the database, safe from prying eyes, but not mine. I spent months searching for Joseph and picked up a thing or two.

I retrieve the co-ordinates. It's a place I know in an old derelict part of town out past the built-up area of Maitland. I hand the information to Theo.

"Your lady is here. Well this is where the message was sent from." I stand up to get the drinks and head back outside to play with my son.

"Holy fucking shit." I hear Dominic growl.

"Damn, Nico. I think I love your woman." Theo's voice is filled with relief.

I chuckle when I hear Nico snarl, telling him to fuck off, get off his ass and go and find his own woman.

I may have just helped him find his woman or at the very least, led him to a place which will give him more clues about where she is. Fingers crossed, he'll find her soon.

I place the drinks on the outside table, scan the backyard and watch as Joseph and Evie laugh and play happily.

For the first time in a long time, I feel a warmth spread over me. Over every limb of my body to settle deep in my heart. I feel so much lighter. I've been given the chance to rewrite my own story and have the happy ending my son and I deserve.

Until we meet again but for now this is The End!!!

Thank you for reading Petal Mine 3.5 and I hope you enjoyed Nico & Josie's story and the brief glimpse you got into the world of the Grasso men if you want more make sure you check out the rest in the series starting with Book 1 ~ Angel Mine.

Do you believe in Love at first sight?

Kay Maree

xx

Available across all platforms

Angel Mine (Mine #1) ~ Dominic & Brooklyn
Kitten Mine (Mine #2) ~ Antonio & Katherine
Sugar Mine (Mine #3) ~ Sergio & Kirsty
Petal Mine (MIne #3.5) ~ Nico & Josie (Ebook Only available in
Essentially Australian)
Trixie Mine (Mine #4) ~ Theo & Trinity (Coming Soon 2018)

Other books by Kay Maree

Shadow Game
Majestic (Midnight Crest Book 1)
Cherry Christmas ~ A Stone Brothers Trilogy

Follow Links

Facebook - @KayMareeAuthor **Twitter** - MisKay85
Insta - miskay

https://www.facebook.com/groups/AngelsKittensSugars/

https://kaymareesmutlover.wixsite.com/contemporary-romance